Peter Cohen

OLSON'S MEAT PIES

Pictures by Olof Landström

Translated by Richard E. Fisher

R&S
BOOKS

Stockholm   New York   London   Adelaide

This is Olson. Olson has a meat pie factory. Olson has been baking his delicious meat pies for thirty years. Olson's meat pies are famous.

Olson uses only the finest ingredients in his pies: the tenderest meat, the freshest onions, the daintiest mushrooms, and the choicest seasonings.

There's always a lot to do at
Olson's factory.

Hugo runs the grinder, and
Olson tastes the mixture.

He wants to be sure it tastes
really good.

Strom, the bookkeeper, is in
charge of the money.

Sometimes Olson goes for a walk. Everyone always greets him kindly. Because, when they see Olson, the first thing they think of is his wonderful meat pies.

When the factory is really busy, Mrs. Olson and the children help out. And once in a while, when it's really *really* busy, Strom, the bookkeeper, has to jump in. "After all, people *must* have their meat pies!" says Olson. They work way into the night.

But one morning, when Olson gets to the factory, he notices that something is wrong.

"Olson, Olson!" yells Hugo. "Strom, the bookkeeper, has run away and he took all the money with him!"

At first, Olson thinks about calling the police. But then he remembers how nice Strom usually is. In fact, they are really good friends. Better not to make a fuss.

Strom will surely come back, thinks Olson.

But a whole week goes by, and Strom, the bookkeeper, is still missing.

Olson can no longer pay Hugo.

He has to run the grinder himself.

And now the fine ingredients are beginning to run out.

Olson goes to the bank and takes out his savings. But he can't afford to buy the tenderest meat, the freshest onions, the daintiest mushrooms, or the choicest seasonings.

The meat pies don't taste quite as good as they used to. Olson hopes no one will notice.

Olson begins to run out of money.

He has to buy even cheaper ingredients. People in the town are saying that Olson's meat pies don't taste the way they used to. And the fewer meat pies people buy, the worse things are for Olson, of course. Pretty soon his money is all gone.

He empties the pockets of all his coats and jackets. His children empty their piggy banks.

Olson buys some tough old hens. He tries to make them go further by adding potatoes and breadcrusts. But that's not enough.

Olson pulls all the leftovers out of the pantry: some old pancakes, a glob of spinach, cold porridge, pea soup, a little rice pudding, and a few fried herring. And when that's *still* not enough, he dumps in a lot of potato peels.

But the grinder needs even more ingredients. Finally, Olson is so desperate that he tosses in just about anything.

First he throws in all his wooden spoons. Then the dishcloths and kitchen towels, some potholders, gloves with no mates, potted plants, old schoolbooks. He throws in clothes: scarves and caps, socks and underwear. In the end, he sacrifices his shirt and his almost-brand-new shoes.

But now the people in the little town have had enough.

Olson's once so loved meat pies just aren't edible anymore.

One morning, everyone gathers outside Olson's factory. They scream and shout:

OLSON'S MEAT PIES JUST WON'T DO!
WE WON'T EAT THIS AWFUL GOO!

People are waving the different things that they have found in their meat pies.

My goodness, they really seem upset, thinks Olson. What am I going to do? If only they weren't so angry.

Suddenly he has an idea!

If they find *nice* things in their meat pies, maybe they won't care so much about the taste!

Mrs. Olson and the children help him. They look in every nook and cranny. They look in every box. Pretty soon they have a whole pile of things.

The next morning, Olson tucks something into nearly every meat pie.

Soon it's rumored that Dr. Bloom has found a watch, the blacksmith a real gold earring, and the minister a little wind-up monkey.

There's a rush of customers.

Wherever you look, people are digging through meat pies.

Everyone wants to try his luck.

But there still isn't much money for new ingredients, because Olson has been forced to lower his prices considerably.

When Olson takes his evening walk,
he becomes awfully sad.
  Everywhere he goes, he sees
discarded meat pies.
  Olson's once so delicious
meat pies lie picked apart
in the gutter.
  And what am I going
to do when I run out of
objects? he wonders.

  Olson can't sleep.
  He thinks of the days
when his meat pies graced
the finest dinner tables.

Suddenly there's a knock on the window!

It's Strom, the bookkeeper!

"Sorry to bother you so late," Strom mumbles.
"But I decided to come back . . . If you'll have me."

And Strom, the bookkeeper, describes how he ran away with all the money.

How he went to the coast to lie on the beach and have a good time for the rest of his life.

But how cold the water was, how boring everything seemed after the first few days, and how lonely he felt.

Strom, the bookkeeper, tells them how one day, to cheer himself up, he bought an Olson meat pie. But it tasted terrible, and he almost swallowed a toy soldier.

He realized then that it was all his fault, and how much his conscience was bothering him.

Strom has brought almost all the money back with him.

Since he is a very thrifty bookkeeper, he has only spent seventeen dollars and twenty-three cents.

The very next morning, Olson sets out to buy new ingredients.

He buys the tenderest meat, the freshest onions, the daintiest mushrooms, and the choicest seasonings.

Hugo is back running the grinder.

Strom, the bookkeeper, is in charge of the money.

Olson tastes the mixture.

He wants to be sure it tastes really good.

The people in the little town are buying more meat pies than ever. They say the pies have never been as delicious as they are now. But they still talk about the time when you could find the strangest things in Olson's meat pies.

Rabén & Sjögren Stockholm

Translation copyright © 1989 by Richard E. Fisher
Illustrations copyright © 1988 by Olof Landström
Originally published in Sweden by Rabén & Sjögren
under the title *Olssons Pastejer,* text copyright © 1988 by Peter Cohen
Library of Congress catalog card number; 88-13812
Printed in Singapore/Polex Int. AB
First edition, 1989
Second printing, 1990
ISBN 91 29 59180 5

R & S Books are distributed in the United States of America
by Farrar, Straus and Giroux, New York;
in the United Kingdom by Ragged Bears, Andover;
and in Australia by ERA Publications, Adelaide